To Cameron!

M A X
for
President

Jarrett J. Krosoczka

MAX ★★★ for ★★★ President

★ Jarrett J.★ Krosoczka ★

Dragonfly Books ⎯⎯⎯ New York

A special acknowledgment to
Robin Bahr Casey and Nancy Galicki
for all their dedication to student government

Copyright © 2004 by Jarrett J. Krosoczka

All rights reserved. Published in the United States by
Dragonfly Books, an imprint of Random House Children's Books,
a division of Random House, Inc., New York. Originally published
in hardcover in the United States by Alfred A. Knopf, an imprint
of Random House Children's Books, a division of Random House, Inc.,
New York, in 2004.

Dragonfly Books with the colophon is a registered trademark
of Random House, Inc.

Visit us on the Web! www.randomhouse.com/kids

Educators and librarians, for a variety of teaching tools, visit us at
www.randomhouse.com/teachers

Library of Congress Cataloging-in-Publication Data
Krosoczka, Jarrett.
Max for president / Jarrett J. Krosoczka.
p. cm.
Summary: Max and Kelly both want to win the election for
class president, but when one of them loses,
the winner finds a way to make the loser feel better.
ISBN 978-0-440-41789-7 (pbk.)
[1. Elections—Fiction. 2. Winning and losing—Fiction.
3. Schools—Fiction.]
PZ7.K935Max 2004
[E]—dc21
2008277134

ISBN 978-0-375-82428-9 (hardcover)
ISBN 978-0-375-92428-6 (lib. bdg.)

MANUFACTURED IN CHINA

12 11 10 9 8 7 6 5

Mrs. Antonio announced that it was time to elect a new class president.

president

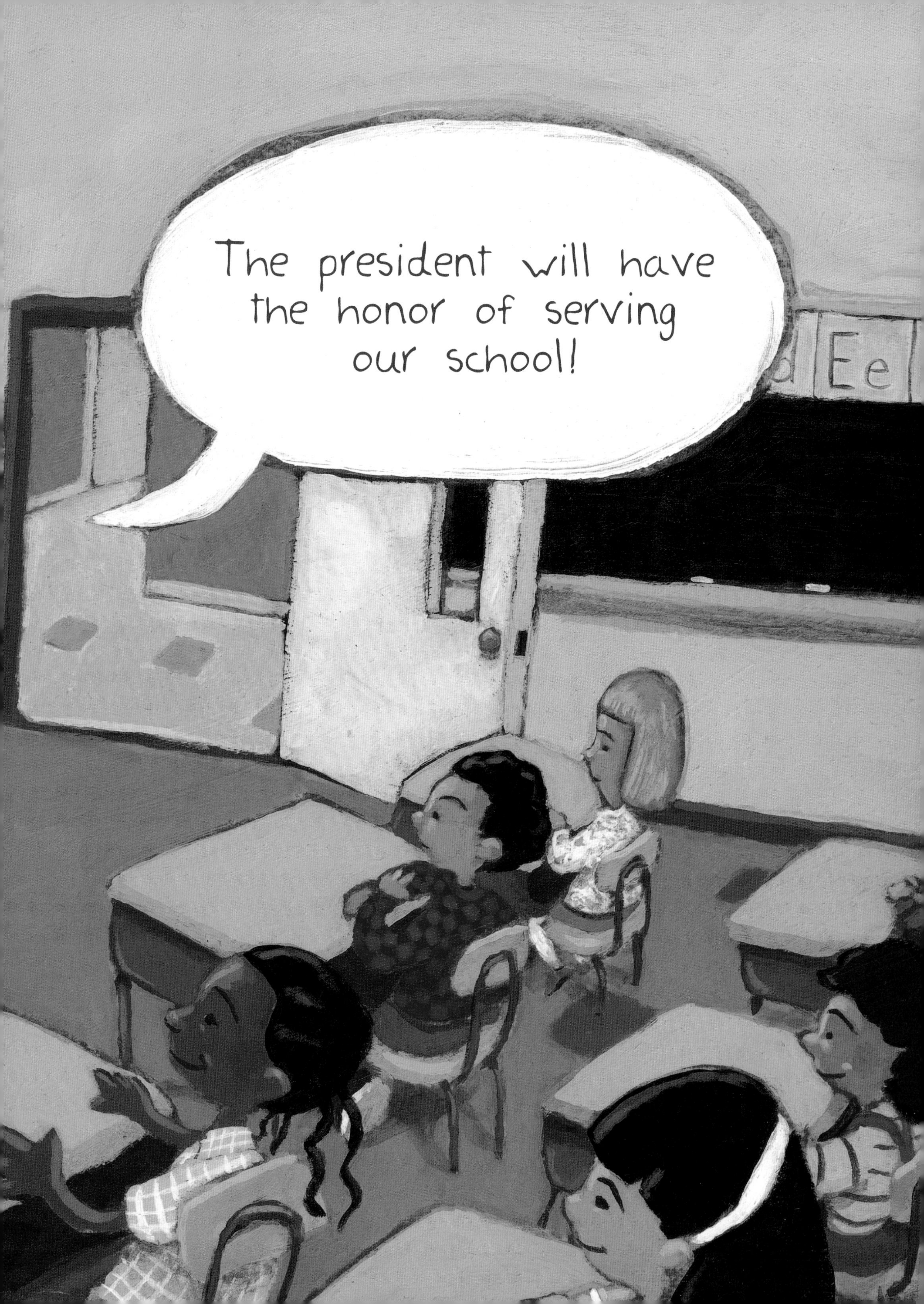
The president will have the honor of serving our school!

MAX thought that he would like to be class president.

So did
KELLY.

Max made signs that said

"Max for President."

Kelly made signs, too.

Max made buttons and gave them
to all of his classmates.

So did Kelly.

Max made promises.

If I'm elected class president, I will work to have better indoor recesses and more exciting games in the game room!

Kelly made promises, too.

Vote for me and we will have more exciting morning announcements and better school lunches.

The time came to vote. Every
student could only vote
for one candidate—
Max or Kelly!

Vote for one
□ Max
□ Kelly

Max waited anxiously.

So did Kelly.

After the ballots were collected and counted, Mrs. Antonio announced the winner.

And the new class president is . . .

Kelly cheered.

Max didn't.

Kelly knew that she needed a good vice president to help get work done. She thought for a second and then asked . . .

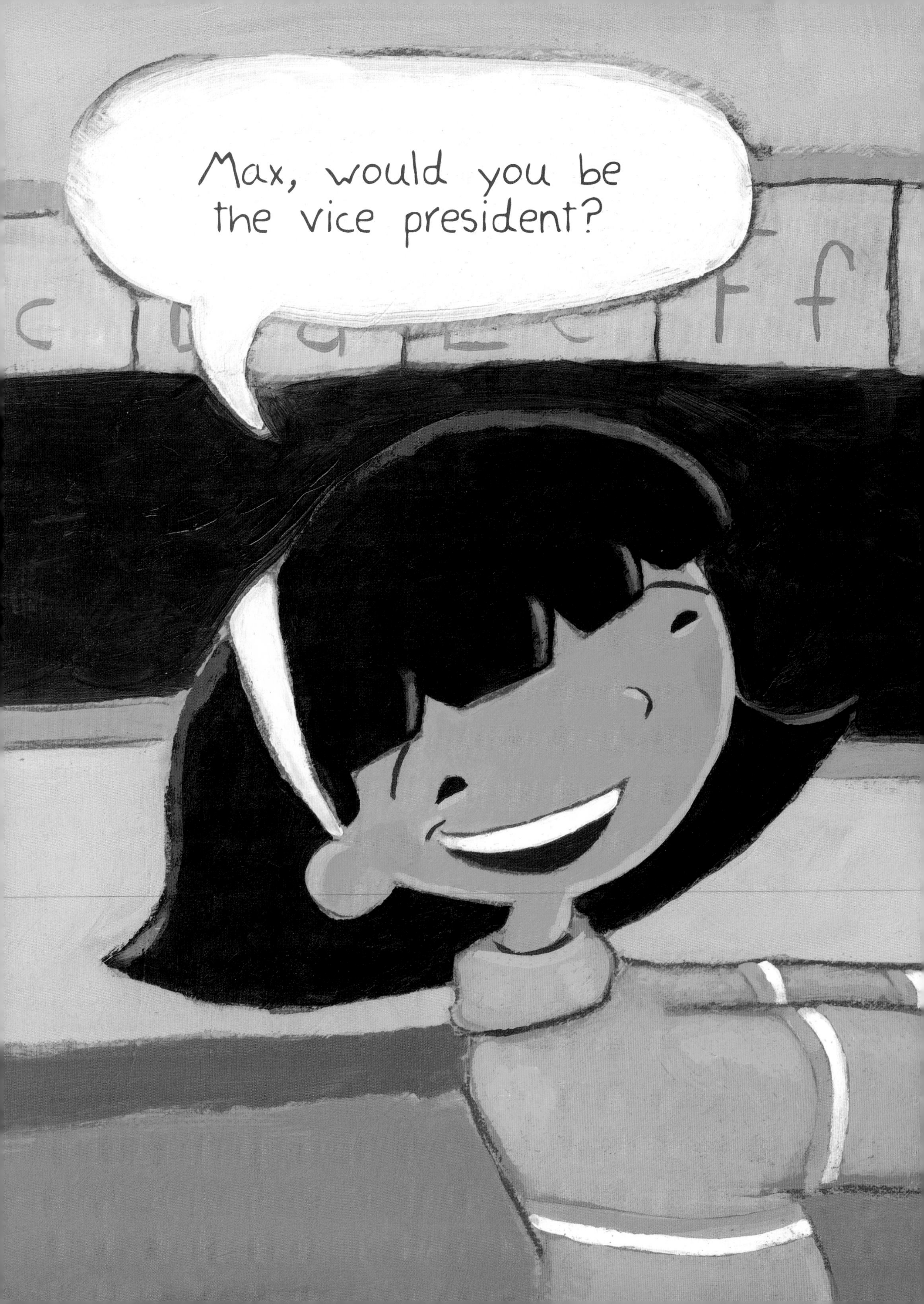
Max, would you be the vice president?

And from then on, both Kelly and Max worked hard to make their school a better place.

Friday is PIZZA DAY
$1 per slice
Help buy new games
for the game room!!!
Mamma G's

The End